How I Became a Horror Writer
A Krampus Story

ALSO BY M. RICKERT

The Shipbuilder of Bellfairie
You Have Never Been Here
The Memory Garden
The Mothers of Voorhisville
Holiday
Map of Dreams

LUCKY GIRL
HOW I BECAME A HORROR WRITER
A KRAMPUS STORY

M. RICKERT

A TOM DOHERTY ASSOCIATES BOOK

NEW YORK

LUCKY GIRL: HOW I BECAME A HORROR WRITER, A KRAMPUS STORY

Copyright © 2022 by M. Rickert

Cover design by Faceout Studio
Cover photographs © Shutterstock.com

A Tordotcom Book
Published by Tom Doherty Associates
120 Broadway
New York, NY 10271

www.tor.com

Tor® is a registered trademark of Macmillan Publishing Group, LLC.

ISBN 978-1-250-81734-1 (ebook)
ISBN 978-1-250-81733-4 (trade paperback)

First Edition: 2022

To Kristen Barrows and Edie Swensen
Even hundreds of miles cannot carve distance between true
friends—I really am lucky

Monsters are real, and ghosts are real too.
They live inside us, and sometimes they win.

Stephen King

Lucky Girl

How I Became a Horror Writer
A Krampus Story

"Listen," Adrienne said. "I have to tell you, I stole it."

We laughed.

"No. Really."

Keith tilted his head to consider the blossom of red tissue paper in his lap, as if it might have teeth, before lifting the final sheet and, with a grin, raising the coffee mug for us to see its logo, "Dell's Diner," and we laughed again.

"I love it."

"Look inside."

He peered into the mug and pulled out a five-dollar bill.

"'Cause I didn't spend it on your gift."

"Perfect. It's just what I need."

I didn't doubt him. Though the five of us had only met weeks earlier, it was easy enough to assess that at least three of our party were not unaccustomed to being short of cash.

The way Keith set the mug down like it was made of rare glass instead of sturdy dinerware conveyed how serious his appreciation was, as did the way he flattened the five-dollar bill then folded it in half and in half again to form a neat square he tucked into the inside pocket of his overcoat, thrown across the back of the couch as though to keep close in case of need for a hasty escape.

Lena began to pick up the discarded wrapping paper, but I told her to stop; I liked the festive atmosphere it brought to my dismal space. My tree had two boards nailed at a cross to the trunk to help it stay upright because, O. Henry–like, I could afford either a tree or a stand, but not both. No lights on the drying branches, but a string bravely hung between tacks on the wall.

"I like what you did with that," Grayson said earlier when he arrived with a package wrapped in silver paper, topped with an elaborate bow and sprig of holly, all of which I suspected must have cost close to the allotted five-dollar limit we had agreed on. What could be inside? I wondered. A stick of gum?

No, as you might already have guessed, not gum but a necklace: a gold chain from which hung the name in script, Adrienne.

She said she loved it, and might actually have meant it, though I was dubious about the validity of her claim of "fat fingers" (clearly they weren't) preventing her from working the clasp. I moved to help, but Grayson beat me to it, lingering longer than necessary over the curve of her thieving neck.

Ridiculous, I thought, to be jealous of a gift like that, or the man who would give it but, to be fair, I was also jealous of Keith's mug and, perhaps most of all, the five-dollar bill. It is not an easy thing to maintain a generous spirit within a season of abundance when one has so little. It wasn't for me, at least.

Grayson thanked Lena with great exuberance for the cap she'd knit in red and white stripes, the colors of our alma mater, but it couldn't have been lost on her that he returned it to its box without even bothering to go through the charade of modeling it. I might have felt a little sympathy had she not so quickly abandoned the book I'd given her, a nearly perfect edition of *Danse Macabre* I'd found in Avol's bookstore on State Street.

Keith's gift to me was as humble as his demeanor, a simple ornament, a deer carved in wood that I immediately hung on my poor tree nearly devoid of decoration. "It's fucking great," I said.

His fair complexion, lightly sprinkled with freckles, brightened with a faint blush beneath my gaze before he nodded curtly, and looked away. Up to that point I'd felt a frisson of attraction between us. I wondered what I had done to make him so uncomfortable. When I realized it was probably the swearing it was all I could do not to laugh.

It was a strange Christmas menu and yet remains one

of my favorites. How delicious it all tasted: the cheap wine, the salty crunch of potato chips atop a creamy bed of noodles, romaine lettuce coated with blue cheese dressing, and sweet potato casserole. The rickety table— left behind by previous tenants—barely tilted, with a Christmas card tucked under one leg. How cheerful the world looked in a kitchen filled with laughter and gift wrap and ribbons and, as darkness crept in—when we returned to my cramped living room—how lovely the light strung across the wall, as though the cracks there had potential for illumination.

"It's just so weird to think of Dell's closing," Lena said, eyeing Keith's mug as she paused before him perched on the sagging couch, to offer her homemade cookies on a decorative plate.

I had been a frequent patron of the small diner wedged between hairdresser and boutique, so snugly nestled it could have been the original source for the term "a hole in the wall." Once a beloved college hangout, it had changed owners several times during my four years at UW. The food and service just kept getting worse, but I liked that I could sit at a table for hours, simply ordering coffee and toast, while writing the stories my classmates enthusiastically excoriated as "twisted fairy tales" and "morally corrupt." In January of my senior year, a new place with a funky atmosphere opened across the street and by that November, Dell's announced it would close at the end of the month.

We met there, eyeing each other across the narrow space from our separate tables, hunched over various stages of the Thanksgiving special, a glop of mashed potatoes, slabs of turkey that looked cut from a loaf, wet bread stuffing, and limp green beans, all coated with oily gravy. What someone like Adrienne (sitting alone at the small table beneath the window, wearing dark glasses and a scarf around her neck as if a spy) was doing in Dell's, I couldn't guess, though, after Keith introduced himself and suggested we all sit together to make a holiday out of it, she confessed to be recovering from a bad breakup. The conversation was awkward, as might be expected amongst strangers, loosened eventually by the wine Grayson graciously ordered. He was quite gregarious. Charming in a way I found off-putting. He said he'd been a frequent patron of Dell's and had come to "pay his last respects," which I thought was an odd way of phrasing it, though I suppose that's what we were all doing. I didn't recognize him, but thought Keith looked familiar. He, however, said he'd never been there. I mentally scolded myself to work on my powers of observation. A writer has to be aware. Lena shared that her plans to spend the day with a co-worker and her husband had fallen through when they both came down with the flu. I wasn't sure I had much in common with any of them, but all of us had remained in Madison after graduation while our classmates moved elsewhere, and I harbored a secret hope we would form the sort of intense, almost familial union I'd seen in friendships depicted in movies.

As a struggling writer I was used to crossing things out, making adjustments, reconsidering where the story was going. That Christmas, after the delicate bubble of conviviality we created over dinner seemed to have been burst by relocating to the living room, when even the relentlessly chirpy Lena had gone quiet, I gave up expectations for our future. All I wanted was to get through the night.

"I wonder where we'll be next year," Lena sighed.

"I know!" Adrienne said, loudly, like a contestant certain of a prize. "Let's do this again."

"I'm not sure what my circumstances will be," Grayson said.

"Well, me either," Adrienne snapped, her eyes narrowed like someone doing computation.

I shrugged as if it didn't really matter before biting into a cookie, a delicious little spice bomb of clove, ginger, and cardamom.

"Who knows where any of us will be?" Adrienne said. "But let's make a game of it. Let's exchange names again. We can do it tonight."

"I don't know about that." Keith sipped from his wine-glass like a professor considering an overly enthusiastic student's proposal. "I'm not sure I will remember."

"You can remember." There was a tone in Adrienne's voice that made me decide not to argue. I guess others heard the same thing because we all agreed, and the pact was set before we even understood its parameters.

"The thing is," she said, "the fun part is, whatever we give, it has to be stolen."

"Oh, I don't know. I mean I can't . . ." Lena stammered.

"Don't be a baby," Adrienne scolded. "I'm not talking grand theft auto. It doesn't have to be anything extreme. It's just a game."

And so it was agreed. It was left to me to write down each name on narrow strips of paper I folded and dropped into the red bowl I'd bought at a summer garage sale, thinking it looked cheerful. When I looked up from my work I realized that, while I had been preoccupied, something had changed in the atmosphere. It took me a minute to figure it out, the way Grayson leaned toward Adrienne, the way Keith paused with the glass at his lips to smile at something Lena said, the way she blushed.

"Here, let me get this out of your way." I tugged at Keith's overcoat. Much of it was hanging off the back of the couch by that point, but he sat against the rest.

"Sorry," he said. "I didn't mean—"

"No, it's not a problem. I'll just put it in the closet. So nothing gets spilled on it." I tugged harder and he leaned forward.

"Really, I can take it." He extended his hand. I gave him the bowl, instead.

After I'd hung up his coat, we picked the names, which each of us carefully secreted in purse or pocket and then, because it was too soon to declare Christmas over, I suggested we tell ghost stories, surprised to learn that none of them had ever done so as part of their family celebration.

Lena, who was a kindergarten teacher, told an unremarkable tale involving the ghost of a calico cat. Keith told a surprisingly gruesome story about an abusive couple whose son soothed himself to sleep every night by imagining terrible ways for them to die, only to answer the door, one Christmas Eve, to a priest and a policeman who reported that the parents—who had gone shopping—had been T-boned by a drunk driver and were dead. The story ended with a chilling conclusion. "He tried to hide his happiness because he knew how he was expected to respond to the tragedy, but that night, even though he slept in a different town, in a different house, in a different bed, his parents found him, reaching through the dark with bloody fingers, poking until his tears were real."

I wondered if I had misread Keith when I thought he was too fussy to be taken seriously. I didn't realize I was staring at him until his eyes locked with mine. Something flashed beneath his placid gaze before his attention was drawn by Lena who patted his arm in a consoling manner. Adrienne, apparently as comfortable with breaking rules as making them, refused to tell a story and insisted I go next. "After all, you're the writer," she said. But writing is different than raconteuring, or at least it always has been for me. Besides, I realized that I had taken us too close to wounds I did not want to open. Rather than share my Christmas ghosts, I made up a rambling account of spirits that spill sugar, tip over teacups, and blow on candles causing flames to flicker in still rooms—all sorts of nonsense. There was no protagonist or antagonist. It wasn't even a story, and when I finished I felt the weight of disappointment, relieved when the collective gaze turned to Grayson.

I'd come to some conclusions about Grayson. Watching him as he crossed his legs and leaned back into the creaking chair to swirl the cheap wine I'd served in the Goodwill glass, as though it were expensive brandy, I doubted he had ever experienced discomfort. He was quite charming, with his dimples and grace, and the box of expensive chocolates he'd presented as a hostess gift that I immediately hid in the cupboard. What was the cost of such ease in the world, I wondered. I bet it cost a lot.

"It's not really a ghost story," he began. "Do you know about the Krampus? The monsters that terrorize households in the midst of their Christmas cheer?" he asked, surveying the room with a regal turn of his head.

"Yes," Lena said in a happy-to-be-a-good-student tone of voice. "Last year, when I was in Chicago with my parents, we went into some store. What was the name again? Well, it doesn't matter. They were selling cards like that. St. Nicholas with horrible creatures . . ."

"Krampus," Adrienne corrected.

"Why anyone would want that on their Christmas cards, I don't know."

"It's quite common in some parts of the world," Grayson said. "My father, for instance, maintained many of the old traditions. I was raised with the threat of Krampus at every St. Nicholas Day's approach. I was frightened of them well before I ever understood their true horror. The story I'd like to tell is about that, if it's all right?"

He looked at me, one eyebrow raised, as if I would ever have any power over a person like him.

"Yes, of course," I said. "Does anyone need a refill before we start?"

After glasses were replenished, and Lena's cookies

passed around once more, I asked if everyone was comfortable. They all said they were, but when I went into the bedroom and returned with a pillow and quilt for myself, the others admitted a slight chill. I stripped my meager bed to furnish blankets for all but Grayson, who waited out the lengthy interruption as though accustomed to a world where those who listened to him sought preparation.

Yet when we were finally cocooned and ready, he leisurely sipped his wine, allowing the silence to fill with expectation.

"The family home, many years before my grandfather bought it, had been a chocolate factory. He got it for a steal, or at least that's what I have been told, though he sank so much money into the remodel it ruined his marriage. As an act of contrition, he built a small church on the property, but it didn't work and she left him. No one ever saw her again. The only evidence of her existence, beyond her progeny, is the garden which flourishes in her absence. Some say she sneaks into the yard to pull weeds and prune dead leaves. Either her or her ghost. That's what people say.

"By the time I made my appearance in the manse, Jovy—he was our man for the yard—maintained the estate as well as any mortal could. What fond memories I have of summers scented with rosemary, basil, and mint!

But this is a winter story. For me, the perfume of winter will always be woodsmoke, pine, and the cherry vanilla tobacco of Jovy's pipe as he walked about, attending to the ravages of snow and ice. I used to trail him while he worked. I was an only child, and even then, in some peripheral fashion aware of the privileges of my life, I did long for companionship. Perhaps that is why I formed a friendship with Mrs. Shellern, the cook who kindly pretended to take my advice about seasoning the stuffing and sugaring the fruit pies.

"She told me how things used to be, how my mother always ordered swags of evergreen draped around the large church doors, and over the stained glass windows, careful to get the ones with holly leaves and berries so the cedar waxwings would join in the celebration. Once she began to tell me how my mother didn't believe the things that had been said about my father before they married, but stopped in midsentence, and made the sign of the cross. Later, I attempted to mimic the gesture in the presence of my father, who whipped me soundly for it then made me promise I would have nothing to do with the church, or Mrs. Shellern.

"'You should not have bothered her,' he said. She was not family or friend. 'You must be polite,' he admonished, 'but never mistake a servant for a companion.'

"I didn't have a chance to correct the relationship,

however, because the next morning there was a new woman in the kitchen who turned her back on me whenever I approached. I was not completely surprised by Mrs. Shellern's absence. It happened frequently that help disappeared, often leaving what little they owned behind.

"Later, when I found Jovy taking a pipe break beside the little church, I asked if he knew where Mrs. Shellern had gone, but he only shook his head as if I had said something solemn. I asked if he knew why they left the way they did.

"Jovy looked over his shoulder at the snow untrammeled by any footprints other than our own. All that could be seen of my father's house was the tip of chimney over the hill. We were in no danger of being heard, yet, in the end, he told me to go play and not worry about ghosts.

"Oh, yes, did I forget to mention? They say the house is haunted.

"That Christmas Eve, I awoke with the light of a full moon fallen across my pillow and, summoned to my window by a strange noise, observed a figure walking across our yard. I thought I'd been bewitched. I probably wasn't supposed to know about such matters, but Mrs. Shellern had told me about witches and their bedevilment. At any rate, I endeavored to open the heavy window, finally achieving a slight lift through which poured the icy air and a metallic sound that arose from the figure I assumed was Santa Claus, walking over the hill.

"I hurried into my socks, slippers, and sweater. I left the warm fire of my room for the cold dark hallway, making careful passage down the stairs, past all our Christmas trees, unlit at that hour, pausing to slip into my boots, put on coat, mittens, and hat.

"The snow was not yet deep, nor was it fresh. It was easy enough to run across it, like an animal freed from its trap. There was a blue quality to the light, I remember that, and how the air stung. I remember, so clearly, the sense of wonder I felt, trekking across the yard, following footprints which led me down the hill to the side of the church, and a small service door I had never noticed from which keys dangled in the lock. It was a surprisingly heavy door, and took some effort, but I did not question what I was doing until I found myself in a narrow darkness so different from the vast one I'd left behind. Years later, when I read the Edgar Allan Poe story, I was reminded of my own beating heart and the way it seemed to echo in the chamber, betraying my presence.

"I soon came to realize I was walking down the narrow passage, into the bowels if you will, below the forbidden church. The way was lit by beeswax candles affixed to sconces; their honey scent sweetened the dank, but their flames illuminated crude depictions on the stone walls of the Krampus in all their grotesquerie of fiendish fangs, brutal horns, drooping tongues dripping with saliva.

"I might have made a hasty retreat had I not, just then, spied a glint of silver on the dirt floor, a jingle bell which I quickly shoved into my pocket as I tiptoed towards the gaping maw of light that signified a wider passage or hall of some kind and, as I did, the odor changed from honey-sweetened dank to putrid.

"'Santa?' I whispered, stupidly, stepping into the hall and seeing everything at once.

"It was a room filled with Krampus, painted and drawn on the walls. Ugly, frightening creatures as big as bears but with horns like goats and hooves like horses, with gaping mouths, claws that carried whips and sticks, and amongst all of them there was one that turned and let out a roar. It leapt towards me, the whip raised, and I ran on my young, swift feet through the narrow way, followed by the lumbering steps and the crashing sound of bells, up from the light to the dark, and out the door where the keys still hung. I hesitated, but no sooner had I turned them than the thing was pounding on the door. I ran through the snow, and up the hill, terrified I would be caught. Not feeling safe even when I entered my house, or crawled, shivering, into bed. I assured myself that my pounding heart, the cold on my face, the Krampus—all of it—had only been a nightmare, but when I closed my eyes I saw more. Chains and locks and, in the corner of the lair, Mrs. Shellern in a cage, reaching for me with a bony hand, her mouth a silent gape.

"I stared into the dark until my eyes burned, then slept so deeply that the light was high when I awoke on Christmas morning."

"So it was a dream?" I asked, barely concealing my disdain. It had been a good effort. Better than mine, without a doubt, but everyone knows a dream is not a story worth telling.

Grayson shrugged. "That's what I wondered. So, later, after gifts were opened and our breakfast eaten, while my father napped by the fire, I decided to investigate. I was surprised when I found Jovy outside, wearing his work clothes. We tried to give the help at least some semblance of a holiday, but there he was, looking quite tired, carrying his toolbox. I wished him a Merry Christmas as he passed, and he nodded in return. I took my new sled down the hill, but it did not travel swiftly as I hoped and I felt foolish for trying. I approached the church with trepidation, only to discover that, in fact, the side wall was made of stone. There was no door.

"How can I describe what I felt? I was old enough to be aware of my good fortune. The Christmas tree, that morning, looked like it grew from a hill of gifts. I opened so many presents I grew weary and didn't finish. Breakfast had been an enormous spread of fruits and bread, pastries and jams, candies and cakes, all just for the two of us. Because I'd briefly mused aloud once that I thought it would be fun to do so, the house decorations that year included a fawn allowed to roam free in the great hall.

"But nothing meant more to me than that wall where the door to the monster's cavern had been. I tilted my face up to the sky, the way I'd seen people in movies do when they were feeling grateful, and was in that state when thunder crashed and snow began to fall. I don't believe I would have had the language to articulate it then, but I think it was the first time in my very privileged life that I felt truly grateful.

"There was no door. There were no Krampus. Mrs. Shellern was not trapped in a cage, begging for my help.

"Relieved to be returned to the world as I thought it was, I slipped my hand into my pocket and felt the hard sphere of proof, the jingle bell etched around its border with holly, which, dangling from my fingers, emitted a single bright ring and I heard something that sounded very much like a scream, suffocated by the wall between us. I stripped off my glove to muffle the clapper then ran, leaving my new sled to be buried beneath snow and forgotten until spring. Back in my room, I used masking tape to wrap the bell within my glove so it could cause no more trouble, then placed it in my pencil box which I tucked into the back corner of my drawer."

We waited while Grayson sipped his wine. His apparently unflappable demeanor looked flapped, however, when he lowered the glass.

"The end," he said.

"Wait. What?" Lena squealed. "What happened next? Did you see the Krampus again? What about poor Mrs. Shellern?"

"It's fiction," Adrienne said. "Not true."

"But what does it mean?" Lena asked.

"Mean?" Grayson shook his head. "It doesn't mean anything."

My guests unwrapped from their blankets to retrieve coats and hats, scarves and purses. They retrieved empty casserole dishes and crumb-littered plates. From the kitchen, I watched Keith pick up a red bow and plop it atop Lena's curly hair, where it remained while she smiled up at him. I turned away from that saccharine milieu to discover Adrienne and Grayson sharing a gaze of their own, though the energy between them felt sharper, almost cruel.

After they left, I walked to the window overlooking the street below to spy on my little party, the red bow still affixed to Lena's head. I wasn't sure I liked any of them, but they had gotten me through an unbearable day and for that, I was grateful.

~

There are all kinds of ghosts. We talk most about the ones that appear in the dark, less about those who never leave at all but follow a person everywhere she goes. Ghosts that never make a sound but crawl out of dreams like cockroaches surprised with a midnight light turned on by a person whose sleep is haunted, whose days are haunted, whose every hour is haunted, whose own life is a ghost of the one she thought awaited her when she was young, before the monster came to her house.

How quaint! How quaint to trap the ugly thing behind a wall. How pleasant to believe evil can be recognized like that and, once seen, captured without harm.

My family was not so fortunate. There I was, alone on Christmas, and there they were, standing in the other room, beside my sad tree, smiling their ghoulish grins.

"Merry Christmas," I whispered, and raised my glass in a toast which, for a moment, appeared to break the impenetrable space between us. That's my mother, father, little brother, and Sampson, our beagle, who runs toward them with a happy waddle, and I thought maybe I was just a terrible person. Selfish, to want more than I had already been given. Unworthy. "I'm sorry," I whispered to the empty room.

~

A year later, my circumstances had improved, but not as much as I'd hoped. I remained in the old apartment with the affordable rent. The crappy furniture had not been replaced but covered by blankets and throws in cheerful colors. My decorations were not elaborate, but I did have a tree stand and was able to hang lights on the branches instead of the wall. That summer I had scored a humble cache of ornaments at a garage sale, and wondered, as I hung them, who had made the salt dough snowman, and whose "Baby's first Christmas" it was, and what had happened to the family that no longer wanted them. For some, this might seem grim, but for me, it was a wonderful game of story. I saved the carved deer Keith had given me the year before for last, placing it in a prominent position, treasured amongst the rest.

The others appeared to have fared better. They arrived with gaily wrapped packages and dishes composed of expensive ingredients like bacon and Gruyère cheese, though our party was incomplete. Grayson sent a letter of apology for his absence, explaining that his father had fallen ill.

"Is he dying?" I asked Adrienne, who scrunched up her nose as if the question were sour and said, "How should I know?" which is how I came to understand that whatever affection blossomed between them the year before had already rotted.

Not so with Keith and Lena, who arrived in beaming unison and spent much of the afternoon laughing at jokes that made no sense to the two of us outside their narrow circle.

"His father is a tea baron? What is that, anyway?" asked Lena, as she settled on the sagging couch so close to Keith that when he shrugged in response, her shoulders hiked as well.

"I don't know, exactly," I said. "I think it just means he's rich." I cut a glance at Adrienne, but she pretended an unnatural interest in the small plate of olives balanced on her lap.

Six olives, to be exact. Maintaining her figure, I guessed. She certainly did look well put together. Like a mannequin. Honestly, I was surprised she'd graced us with her presence. It seemed to me she would have preferred a celebration with more glitter and less dross.

"When did you learn Grayson wasn't coming?" she asked, later, as I came upon her standing at the makeshift bar in the corner of my kitchen, pouring another glass of wine from the bottle she brought.

"Last week," I said. "He sent the gift for our exchange, and a note with his apologies. Would you like to read it?"

Adrienne shook her head once, quick and abrupt, then

sipped her wine between tightened lips, staring at the wall above the sink as if something ugly grew there.

I decided to leave her to her meditation, only to find Keith and Lena in the midst of a kiss, and honestly I wasn't sure which was the worse element for my gathering, a disgruntled guest who might not even have come had she known her ex wouldn't be there, or lovers so enchanted with each other no one else mattered.

"All right," I said. "Time for the gift exchange!"

"Yes," said Adrienne, coming out of her corner to join us. "Let's find out what sort of thieves you all are."

The gifts revealed some of us better suited to the task than others. Adrienne had Lena's name. She gasped when she opened the package to find a sweater in a lovely shade of lavender that brought out the blue of her eyes. It was just her size too, small like she was, so soft she brought it up to nuzzle against her cheek.

"It's cashmere," Adrienne said.

Lena squealed and pulled the garment from her face to proudly show the tag to Keith.

He apologized as he handed Adrienne her gift, which was a stapler she mutely stared at, causing an uncomfortable atmosphere to settle over the assembled.

Lena, it turned out, had Keith's name, which they laughed about as though nothing so funny had ever happened before in the whole world. She told an elaborate account of how she'd stolen the salt and pepper shakers while he had gone to the bathroom and how frightening it was when he'd come back to their booth intending to finish his meal, but could not find the salt he'd thought had just been there and on and on. Their mutual absorption was broken by moments when Keith glanced my way, out of a sense of polite inclusion, I assumed, before Adrienne and I escaped into the kitchen where she poured wine, with an arched brow, for the both of us.

Upon our return to the happy couple, Lena turned to me. "You're next," she said. "What did Grayson send you?"

I felt I'd been quite mature in resisting the impulse to peek into the package, about the shape and size of a fairy's coffin, which I had placed beneath the tree, beside a small square box wrapped in recycled paper.

I much preferred being the watcher to being the watched, and felt uncomfortable with all eyes on me. The size of the box meant there would be no cashmere sweater for me, but perhaps some expensive chocolates like the kind he'd brought the year before (devoured in bed on Christmas night) or jewelry, though, remembering the name necklace, I hoped for the former. Instead, it was an old pencil box. I had to smile when I lifted the lid.

"What is it?" Lena asked.

A clump of blue material bound by dusty masking tape

which, as expected, did not give at my touch.

"Wait, is that ..." Lena's voice trailed off as I began to pick at the tape.

"Do you need a scissors?" Keith asked.

I thought I might, but just then a good portion pulled apart and the glove released its hold on the round silver bell etched around its perimeter with holly.

"Are you going to ring it?" Adrienne asked.

"Don't," Lena said.

"Why not?" Keith and I asked in unison.

"Don't you remember? What happened? If you ring it monsters come."

Adrienne and I exchanged a knowing look.

"Should we tell her?" I asked.

"Tell me what?"

"Sweetheart, there are no monsters," Keith said.

For the first time I saw Lena look at Keith as if he was unappealing.

"It was just a story," I said. "Maybe his father put on some kind of costume to keep Grayson out of the church; if there even is a real church. More like an old shack, probably. Assuming any of it was true. For all we know Grayson lives in a trailer."

Lena's jaw dropped as she turned from me to Keith and, I swear, I saw her lean away from him a little.

"Sweetheart," Keith pleaded.

"Well, technically, he cheated," Adrienne said. "We all agreed to give something stolen."

"It *is* stolen. It's the monster's bell!"

Adrienne squinted at Lena. "Even if there was a 'monster,' which there wasn't. Obviously. No one stole the bell. It was found."

"But if you find something that belongs to someone else and keep it, that is stealing," Lena said, and I was reminded she was a kindergarten teacher.

"Oh, for god's sake." Adrienne took a large gulp of wine. Keith clapped his hands on his knees as if about to stand.

"Wait. Who had Grayson's name?" Lena asked.

"Me." I had been excited about my clever gift, but it seemed diminished by the cashmere sweater, Keith's obviously corrupt enthusiasm for Lena's stupid salt and pepper shakers, and Grayson's very clever bell.

"What did you send him?"

I got onto my hands and knees to retrieve the small box beneath the tree, which I placed in Keith's lap. He looked up at me in confusion. He had such a pleasant face.

"Open it."

"Didn't you have Grayson's name?"

"Yes, but he's not here, and I think it would be fun for you to open it. Just do it. You'll see why."

He approached it meticulously, which I rather appreciated as it heightened the sense of anticipation. By the end, even Adrienne was leaning forward for a closer look. We were all quiet as he pulled back the layers of tissue paper until he looked up at me and laughed, a great loud Christmas guffaw.

"Well played," he said, holding up the five-dollar bill, folded into a neat square. "I wondered what had happened to it. But how did you?"

I told, in minute detail to rival Lena's salt and pepper chronicles, how I used the opportunity of hanging up Keith's coat the previous year for my little thievery. "Got my Christmas shopping done early," I said, repeating the line I had rehearsed several times, though it fell flat.

There were quite a few jokes about checking pockets and purses as they left, and I was just shutting my door when Lena came running back to press the bill into my palm.

"So you can send it to Grayson," she said, then pivoted away, flicking her small, white-gloved hand in the air as farewell.

"Merry Christmas" and "Thank you" and "Happy New Year," they called but I realized, as I stepped back inside, that we had made no plans for the following year. We weren't really friends, just people who had formed a union out of loneliness.

I shoved the money into my pocket. Grayson certainly didn't need it. His father was a tea baron, for god's sake. I topped off my wine and sat on the sagging couch, staring at the bell in its nested pencil box, as if monitoring it in fear it might ring itself. It sat there, not moving, of course, and yet I could hear its cheerful taunt.

~

I was sixteen. It was December, and the house was decorated in my mother's holiday style, so unrelenting we even had a Christmas toilet seat cover, a smiling Santa Claus with the seat down, mittens covering his eyes when the seat was up. Our tree was lit with the old-fashioned colored lights you might have seen in movies. If a bulb burned out, the whole thing went dark. Sometimes they sparked a little before that happened, which lent a particular thrill to the season.

My father was on the couch, reading the newspaper. My little brother in his room, I suppose, though I really don't know for sure. At that time in my life, I worked to ignore him. My mother was in the kitchen, the chicken in the oven, pots on the stove. Mashed potatoes and roasted chicken was a favorite meal of mine.

"I'll be back," I said, quick-footing around Sampson, who followed me with devotion.

"Where are you going?" It must have been the conflu-
ence of kitchen light against the winter gray beyond the
window that caused my mother's face to look as though
it had already taken on a death pallor.

"I'll be home in time for dinner," I promised, feeling
relief as I stepped into the cold, never guessing how many
times I would return to that moment. When I pulled the
door shut behind me, the Christmas wreath swayed, and
the bell tied to the bow jingled.

~

I was careful with Grayson's bell, holding it immobile
with one finger while tightly taping the glove back on
with the other hand. I returned the muzzled bell to the
pencil box which, just to be careful, I taped shut as well,
before bringing it into my bedroom where I shoved it
into the back corner of a drawer.

You never know when you might want a monster, I
thought.

~

We lost contact for decades but, like many awkward social circles that time and distance once severed, were re-
united on Facebook. Lena and Keith had gotten married.

He looked older and slightly heavier, but his countenance remained pleasant. Lena had maintained a sprite-like appearance—right down to her floppy hats festooned with felt flowers—but, in every photo, appeared worn out, as though recovering from an illness or addiction. Not long after we became friends again (in the Facebook way) poor Lena died in a car accident, which was relayed by Keith with a short tribute film he posted, a montage of photographs: Lena as a baby, toddler, high school graduate, college girl, kindergarten teacher, etc., followed by a series of adorable Keith and Lena moments. At the beach, at the park, at a restaurant, and then their wedding, which had a decidedly hippie vibe about it and, after that, a few more photos, similar to what I had already seen, a tired-looking Lena sitting at what looked to be a kitchen table, kneeling in a garden, staring out from a dark corner with sad, wide eyes as if lost. I wrote a note of condolence, but did not go to the funeral, which I felt certain would be understood. Everyone knew about me. I was the horror writer with an aversion to all things funereal.

I spent many years in obscurity, finding my "voice" as they say and, when I finally accepted that every fairy tale I tried to write would end in mayhem, and every love story was a crime, I embraced my style, dressed in leather, dyed my hair Joan Jett black, and wore rings that made my fingers clatter like claws. By looking at me, you wouldn't guess how often I slept with a light on, or that I preferred romantic comedies to adaptations of my own work.

Adrienne, born too early to be a true "influencer," persisted in sharing yoga poses and tropical vacations interspersed with intimate details about her personal life such as the post about her eating disorder.

"People think this is something you get over, but you don't really. Don't get me wrong. I haven't purged in decades. I eat three meals a day. But every hour I am confronted by the girl I once was who almost died rather than accept her appetite." Her relationship status was listed as divorced. Her employment history threaded with titles that sounded suspect and absurd like, "Executive Innovator of Dynamic You," whatever that meant.

Grayson was one of those people who joined Facebook in order to surveille rather than share. His banner was a colorful sky with nothing on the horizon to indicate location. He kept his friends list private, and never bothered to post any information about employment or relationships. In fact, he never posted anything at all. The only way I knew he was the Grayson I remembered was that he accompanied his friend request with a pleasant, chatty DM about his fond memory of the Christmas we'd spent together, and how pleased he'd been when he recently spied *The Demons Next Door* at the airport bookstore. "You kept me up all night," he wrote.

Though we hadn't spoken for so long, and I wasn't even sure I liked him when we had, Grayson became my new best friend. Not really, of course, but if you want to know the way to earn any writer's affection, it's through the pages they have written.

After his father's death Grayson became the tea baron. He took frequent trips to a plantation in India. "You should visit sometime," he wrote, which I assumed was not meant to be taken seriously.

I assumed the same thing when, that fall, after Lena died, he suggested the four of us have a Christmas reunion.

"I was always sorry I had been unable to attend the second gathering, and then quite disappointed when we lost contact afterwards," he wrote.

While both he and I were orphans, I did not expect Adrienne and Keith to be equally untethered, so I was surprised when, a week later, Grayson wrote to tell me they had accepted his invitation and hoped I would join them at his "estate."

What the hell, I thought, as I packed my bags—if nothing else it would be material for a new story. Four people who barely know each other gathered in a haunted house. I could do something with that, couldn't I? Something original?

A hideous love story? A winter haunting? A yuletide tale of terror?

Or maybe a story about being lost, I thought as I drove down the winding road banked by evergreens, the sky darkening with clouds of promised snow. As much as I welcomed the navigational assistance of GPS, I had been suspicious of it ever since finding myself parked on the side of a road staring at a cornfield after entering the address for a stranger who had invited me to speak to her book club. I used to do that sort of thing before the movies, and the money, came in.

And yes, those experiences were the inspiration for *The Horror Book Club,* the first of my novels to make it on the *New York Times* Best Seller list.

I was surprised to notice a car in my rearview mirror when I'd been the only vehicle on the road for so long, then annoyed as it trailed too close, before swearing with pleasure when I recognized Adrienne, who waved at me as she passed. She signaled to pull over and I wondered, as I did, who sat in the passenger seat, a silhouette as though not fully human. I tucked the image in a corner of my mind for future use, a shadow man like the one who often came into my room during dreams.

It was Keith, though.

We got out of our cars to hug each other with vague embraces as though uncertain we weren't contagious.

Adrienne looked older than her photographs, but smiled at me so broadly, and with such a direct gaze from beneath her perfect eyebrows, I questioned if it was possible her affection was sincere.

Keith kept his arms around me longer than I expected. When he finally stepped back I looked up at him to scrutinize the face I remembered, buried beneath the added pounds and years.

"Hey," he said. "You look different. Good. It's good to see you. The famous writer."

I always found it awkward when anyone commented on my career as though it was something that happened to me rather than something I had struggled to create, but before I could formulate a response Adrienne announced it had begun to snow, as if we were too dense to realize it ourselves.

"We need to get going," she said. "I think we're almost there. This is taking longer than I expected."

I wondered why the two of them had not invited me to join their car pool even though I would have declined any such offer. I didn't really like being in close quarters with people. Still—and I have been this way my whole life—I did like to be asked.

There is little I enjoy more than the encompassing warmth of a heated car on a cold day, listening to music. I checked the rearview mirror and saw darkness closing in, swallowing the long, winding road behind me. I cranked up the heat and, with Adrienne to follow, no longer needing to hear the GPS voice, flicked the radio on, immediately serenaded by bells. It was the season. I had heard many bells already that winter but, perhaps because of where I was, they sounded different. Ominous. I turned it off.

Just like that, the door is opened, and a monster creeps out.

~

I was sixteen and thought I was in the middle of a love story. You are going to roll your eyes when I tell you this next part, but I hope you remember, as my therapist has encouraged me to, I was not a child of the internet age. A lot of what seems obvious now was unheard of when I was young.

Every year my mother spent the weekend after Thanksgiving at the dining room table surrounded by dwindling stacks of our best dishes washed and dried, put away in sprints between her sessions of addressing envelopes. When I was very young I begged to help, but that last November, the begging was reversed. I reluctantly agreed, then shoved aside the crystal butter dish to make a place for myself. My penmanship wasn't great, and we both knew it, but it was the first time I realized my mother's wasn't so great, either. We laughed about that. At first I worked in fancy—the words in red, the numbers in green—that sort of thing, but soon settled on efficiency. Who were all these people anyway? Most of the names were unfamiliar to me. (And I had no idea that I would be meeting many of them, only weeks later, at a funeral decorated with poinsettias and evergreen.) After a while, my mother asked if my hand was getting sore and, even though it wasn't really—she'd been at it a lot longer than I had—we took a hot chocolate break. When it began to snow, she found a station playing Christmas carols, and we sat at the kitchen table together, watching winter come down.

Later that week, the cards started to arrive, some addressed to the family, most addressed to my parents, and, surprisingly, one addressed to me, which I opened in my bedroom, intrigued when a small key fell out onto my lap.

The illustration on the card was of a smiling cartoon bear holding in its little paw a red flower. Inside was a short, handwritten note. He had seen me, he said, at the mall, and wanted to approach, but decided not to when he realized I was in the midst of an argument with my parents.

The embarrassing scene that had caught the stranger's

attention happened two weeks earlier when I begged my parents to let me watch *Carrie* with some friends I'd run into. We were on the way to my grandmother's birthday party and had only stopped to pick up the cake. After they said I couldn't stay, I surprised all of us by having a sort of fit in the middle of the food court. My mother tried to calm me down by saying my name over and over again. When my father took me by the elbow to steer me away, I screamed as if I'd been stabbed in the side, causing an eerie stillness to settle over the holiday shoppers who stared at me until I broke the spell by stomping toward the exit. I was horrified to think I'd been recognized, though certainly not surprised. My weird first name alone might have been enough, but also my father, a high school history teacher in Grafton, bore some renown. With that information it would have been easy to find my address in the phone book. What I couldn't understand was why anyone would have been attracted to such behavior. Every time I remembered it, I felt ashamed.

He thought I was amazing, he wrote. He wanted to meet me.

"Please answer. Leave a note in the mall locker. Use the enclosed key."

In those days there still were things like public space lockers intended for shopping bags and heavy coats. We teenagers had developed less wholesome purposes. There was one key for each locker, but Paul Fellows, who worked at Sears, was very accommodating about making copies. He had only graduated the year before and missed being popular. . . .

That Saturday I told my mother I was going Christmas shopping. She offered to come along, but I told her I wanted to be alone so I could buy her gift.

"It's a big mall," she said. "I'm sure we could find some space."

"Please," I said. "I want to be sure you don't see."

She looked happy, and I felt a glimmer of guilt. Until that year, we had been very close.

I was thrilled when I opened the locker to find another envelope with my name on it, though initially disappointed when the same cartoon bear grinned at me from behind the same red flower before deciding it was probably romantic. Maybe he had bought a box of those cards, all meant for me.

"So happy you came," he wrote. "I hope this means you are interested in meeting me?"

I looked up from the card. Was he watching from behind the pillar at Cinnabon? Was he the red-haired guy wearing a paper hat, handing the wrapped egg roll to the man in the long coat? Could he be the man in the long coat?

"Please come to Red Pine Park on December 16th at 4:30. Meet me at the gazebo. Leave your key inside the locker, if you agree. Otherwise you can throw it away, along with my heart."

I laughed. Funny, I liked that. Sure, even naïve me was beginning to recognize some possible issues but also, though it was growing dark by four thirty in winter, the hour seemed unthreatening as did the location. Red Pine Park was really just a little square surrounded by streets lined with houses. Besides, I wouldn't wait in the gazebo. I wasn't an idiot. I'd wait by the little grove of evergreens. That's how small Red Pine Park was. A person standing at one end of it could see all the way to the other.

I thought I was so clever.

I put the card I'd brought for him inside the locker and placed the key on top of it. I'd taken one of our family cards, a Christmas scene, old-fashioned, the way my mother liked, a little house in the snow, the windows yellow with golden light. In one, I had drawn a face that was supposed to be me but looked slightly terrifying. Beneath the printed "Merry Christmas," after thinking about it for quite a while, I merely signed my name.

Afterward, I wandered the mall, which was elaborately decorated with fake trees, large red balls, and gold bows. Carols blared through the loudspeakers, and the line for Santa Claus was long. I always loved the holiday, but that year felt infused with an extra touch of magic. Who knows, I thought, maybe by New Year's I will have a boyfriend. Maybe I already did!

I fingered the lousy dollar in my pocket that was all I had to my name. Most girls my age made money babysitting, but my business suffered when it got around how I told scary bedtime stories. I stopped at Fanny Farmer's to buy one piece of fairy food, the chocolate-covered candy I loved, which I ate while trying to decide if I was a terrible daughter. Then I walked to the Sears jewelry counter where I pocketed a pair of gold hoop earrings for my mother. I'd seen her looking at some just like them once.

So that is how it came to be that, a week later, as my family was being terrorized and murdered, I was standing in a park with snowflakes melting on my face, thinking how lucky I was. It all looked so beautiful: the falling snow, the colored lights dangling from the gazebo and strung from the eaves of houses surrounding the park, and that feeling of being sixteen with a secret, full of the possibilities of life and the season.

I waited so long that snow began to form a crust on my hat. I wondered if someone had played a trick, setting me up to be mocked, but had seen no one other than a few passing cars and the Barrows family returning with their Christmas tree attached to the roof of their station wagon, the little kids jumping up and down with glee.

I didn't know if my secret admirer was a jerk, or had just run into some kind of issue with getting out of the house—not unheard of at that age—but decided I didn't care. What had gotten into me, anyway? I'd always vowed not to be one of those girls who got silly about boys. I wanted to be a writer. Was I in danger of giving away my dream to someone who sent me a card with a stupid cartoon bear? I'd seen it happen to other girls in my small town. One day Annie Walter was class valedictorian, and the next she was working at the drugstore. Not a single person I knew was living their dream come true, not even my father who talked about the history book he would write someday. I needed to be wary of such distractions, I scolded myself, as I made my way to a place that no longer existed, replaced by a new world where lights spun red over the snow.

I was too naïve, and in a state of shock, to understand the implications surrounding the questions Detective Keller asked me about my absence. I told almost the whole truth. I'd gone to the park, I said, and stayed out longer than expected.

"What did you do?" she asked.

"I just stood there."

"Doing what?"

"Thinking."

No one could doubt my distress, which was massive

and genuine. Several people had seen me standing by the gazebo, which corroborated my alibi. Mrs. Barrows said she'd even considered inviting me to join her family because I looked like an orphan out there. She said it to a reporter, her voice breaking at the end, and the local news played it over and over again.

They said they would get the guy. There was speculation it might have been one of my father's students, but he was genuinely liked, and it wasn't long before the case went cold.

The next Christmas, when I was hanging bargain basement orbs on the tree at my grandmother's house ("It's your house now too," she kept saying) my mind released the memories: the scent of roasted chicken, my mother telling me to be back for dinner, the way the wreath swayed and the bell rang as I shut the door.

"Ro, are you all right?" Grandma asked when I dropped the Styrofoam ornament.

We wept together, but I never told her the specific nature of my grief. How I'd survived the great tragedy of my life because I'd left the family who loved me for a cartoon bear.

It wasn't until years later, when there were several stories about men killing parents and siblings in hopes of having access to a young girl, that I came to believe I was in a Lolita story.

I called Detective Keller to tell her.

"Northridge Mall?" she asked. "That's gone now, you know. Do you still have the cards?"

I didn't. What wasn't lost in the fire was ruined by smoke or water damage. "What about the man?" I asked.

"The one in the long coat?"

"Yeah," I said, hearing how ridiculous it sounded.

"Can you describe his face?"

I could not.

"Listen, Roanoke."

"Call me Ro, please." My affection for my parents had matured, but I had not yet arrived at the point in my life where I appreciated the humor in being named after one of my father's favorite historical mysteries.

"You could be right. I'm not dismissing you, okay? There's a cop I know, years ago, who got a bad feeling about some guy standing in a doorway. Downtown Chicago. He walks by and has that feeling. Finds a reason to walk by again, and that feeling comes up. So the dude tosses his cigarette on the sidewalk and my friend arrests the guy for littering. No shit. He takes him in. Turns out this guy just shot his wife. Come to find out he still had the gunpowder on his hands. My friend smelled it, but it was so subtle, he didn't even realize. Sometimes our brain puts it together before we can fully explain how or why. Maybe you have more information than you thought.

You could be right about the man in the long coat. It's always bugged me how you survived. Let me know if you remember anything else. In the meantime, I don't think you have anything to worry about, if this bear card theory is right."

"Why's that?"

"Oh, you would be way too old for that type now. Consider yourself lucky."

Detective Keller retired a few years ago. The last time I talked to her she said it was one of the greatest disappointments of her career that she had never solved the case, and then we went through a few weird minutes where I comforted her.

A cold case detective took over after that. I talked to him about once a year around the holidays. He never had anything new to share, and my already depleted store of hope was severely challenged by the fact that he couldn't even remember my name and called me Rory.

~

By the time I made the turn into Grayson's driveway (marked by two stone gryphons with wreaths on their heads) it was dark, the snow falling hard. I realized how tense I'd become when I found myself exhaling with relief then immediately swerved on a slick patch. I resisted the urge to brake and released my grasp on the steering wheel, lessons I'd learned in my younger days of driving the crappy Audi. My headlights briefly illuminated Adrienne's distant taillights, the trees, a hulking figure in the forest, and then, as I regained control, the long drive banked by pine, no other vehicle in sight.

I stopped to catch my breath. What was I doing? For years I'd lived with a fear, superstition, maybe premonition that I would die during the Christmas season, as if my survival had been a terrible mistake. I switched on the windshield wipers and continued at a cautious speed. What the fuck, didn't bears hibernate?

I might have turned around. Driven for hours in the dark. Sent an apology text. An unexpected emergency. Or some other lie. If not for the ice, I might have had a different life.

~

Later, after the awkward greeting, the mandatory relinquishing of phones, and a brief respite spent "freshening up" in the exquisitely appointed bedroom, I found myself looking for small cameras hidden within the candelabras (yes, plural) or in the branches of glimmering evergreen trees (plural again) that surrounded us, seated at the white-cloth table, beneath the chandelier. This was a joke, right? No one really lived like this.

"It is done with a crank."

"What's that?" Keith asked.

"I noticed Ro considering the chandelier," Grayson said. "I assumed she was trying to ascertain how we were able to light the candles. Am I right?"

Though it hadn't even occurred to me to wonder, I nodded. The change in Grayson's appearance was as stunning as the surroundings, and every time I looked at him I felt confused.

"A crank lowers it to the table for lighting."

"How many candles are there?" Adrienne asked.

"Thirty. Don't worry. They are quite secure." He locked his gray eyes on me for longer than felt comfortable, then turned to face Adrienne. "I notice you've hardly eaten any of your salad. Can I get you something else?"

Even in the dim light I could see her complexion flush with embarrassment. You might recall my fifth novel, *How to Starve a Ghost*. Because of my research, I know it can be challenging for those recovering from eating disorders to have their appetite commented on. Indeed, Adrienne looked down at her plate like a chastened child.

"I really like this curly stuff," Keith said, stabbing a leaf with his fork. "What is it, again?"

"Frisée." It was hard to read Grayson's face. He'd gained so much weight, the sharp lines absorbed into a doughy complexion, his lips an almost obscene pink portal.

Adrienne was saved from any further scrutiny by the man shuffling into the room, so ancient looking I half expected moths to rise from his shoulders, and had to suppress a giggle when he lifted my plate with an alarming tremor. It was going to be a long night, I thought, if the same pace would be applied to every course, but what of it? The windowpanes shuddered at the storm, while I sat warm and sheltered in a room full of inspiration for horror.

"Keith, are you all right?"

I couldn't decide about Adrienne. One minute I thought she seemed softer, more approachable, and the next she was the girl I remembered, self-absorbed and insensitive, prying Keith's grief for table fodder.

"We don't have to talk about—" I began, but Keith interrupted me.

"Frisée. Why can't I ever remember that word? She used to make fun of me for that."

"Who?" I asked.

"Lena," Adrienne hissed, obviously thinking I was the one being dense.

I didn't know what to say. Certainly I understood the absurdity of grief, how it can arrive on a lettuce leaf, or a cheap Christmas ornament, or a flame. Keith's long fingers caressed the frisée as though it were a lock of Lena's hair.

The room rumbled with the return of our server pushing a noisy cart laden with covered dishes. Even before he uncovered the plates, I knew what it was by the aroma. Oh yes, the absurdity of grief, how it can arrive on a plate like that.

"Roasted chicken," Keith said. "My favorite."

He seemed recovered, the frisée forgotten. He even smiled, his face lit with golden light. I was surprised by his effect on me, but there I was, grinning at Keith, and there he was, looking at me as if I was his happy place.

"Well, isn't this interesting," Adrienne said cutting her chicken with surgical precision.

Keith raised his eyebrow at me. Good. It seemed he agreed. This was all comically strange.

"Chai roasted," Grayson said. "An old recipe from Kerala."

"Kerala?" Keith asked.

The three of us, Adrienne, Grayson, and I answered in unison, "India," which was not such a funny thing, but we laughed, which seemed to elevate the mood. Well, that and the old man refilling our glasses with quivering stealth.

By the time we'd finished dessert (Baked Alaska with a chocolate rum sauce) I don't think any one of us was sober. Grayson suggested we all move into the parlor. Trailing behind, Keith whispered to me, "Morticia Addams awaits you in the parlor," and I giggled.

Grayson turned with surprising grace and smiled, or at least the corners of his lips turned up as he ushered us into the room with his large hand. I noticed, as I passed, that his cologne did not successfully mask the sour odor beneath it. What had gotten into me? Why was I being so mean about Grayson? Was I jealous of his beautiful home? It was another stunning room, decorated in mahogany and red, the focal point a large fireplace with an elaborately carved mantel. I didn't realize I was sulking as I sank into the couch beside Adrienne until she asked if I was all right. I fake-smiled and nodded. What had I been thinking? I was not fit company. Christmas was my wild season, my time for demons, but I looked up from my pout to find Keith staring at me, and changed my mind. Who knows, I thought. Maybe I'll have a happy ending, after all.

"How lovely for us to be together again." Grayson raised his glass in a toast. "To Lena, who is with us in spirit."

How well I knew the never-ending intrusion of condolences. Thinking to change the subject, I opened my mouth but before anything came out, Adrienne said something about the cookies Lena made all those years ago.

"Yes," Keith nodded. "Lebkuchen. This is the first Christmas in a long time when I won't have any."

"A shame." Grayson set his glass on the small, marble-topped table beside his chair. "How unfortunate you decided never to have children."

"We didn't decide."

"Why don't we talk about something else?" I asked.

"I mean," Keith continued in a ragged voice. "She—we—wanted children very much."

"You don't have to talk about this," I said.

"I told her we could adopt."

"Ah, just in time," Grayson heralded the old man's return, shuffling in to fill our glasses. It was my first close look at him, and I was surprised to find kind eyes in that wrinkled face, but when his lips parted slightly in some vague semblance of a grin they revealed unusually sharp eye teeth. Like a vampire, I thought, though I am given to dark speculation wherever I am, especially at Christmas.

"Why don't we tell ghost stories?" Adrienne said. "Like we did the first time we were together."

"Oh, I don't know . . ." I began, thinking the suggestion was insensitive with Lena so recently dead.

"Yes, I'm not sure it would be at all fair," Grayson said. "Considering how Ro is a famous author now."

"I didn't mean—"

"Right. I suppose you have a point." Adrienne frowned at me.

"I must say, I was quite flattered when I read *Silent Night, Unholy Night*. To think my little story had turned into a novel read by thousands!"

How quickly the conversation had veered into uncomfortable territory. It is true that Grayson's story was the inspiration for my first novel, but inspiration is not the same as perspiration, as we writers like to say. I am the one who sat at that rickety table every night after working all day making lattes and cappuccinos and pouring coffee to customer's weird specifications. (One woman always brought in her own mug, a single bean at the bottom, which she instructed me not to lose. Was it a magic bean? I never asked.) I wrote and crossed out and tossed pages into the trash. Me. Not Grayson. I found a novel buried in the incomplete tale he told. I was the one who, after finally finishing the thing, celebrated with a beer, all alone on the fire escape because I'd given up any social life. I was the one who queried agent after agent, and was rejected by some of the best and the worst in the business. I was the one who wept and questioned what I was doing to believe I could be a writer. I mean, how much luck did I expect to be given in life? After all, I was the sole survivor of a home invasion, wasn't that enough?

"Why should I have been surprised?" Grayson asked. "You are quite good at taking what you want, aren't you?"

Not sure I could trust what I might say, I began to plot my escape. Obviously, I couldn't leave in the middle of the storm, but as soon as the roads were clear, I'd find a way out.

"I don't think you're being fair," Keith said, and then, as if he'd read my mind. "I mean, all of us heard that story. Only Ro was able to turn it into a novel."

Grayson inhaled deeply, as though smelling something delicious. "Of course. I don't begrudge your success. Forgive me if I've given the wrong impression."

I nodded and fake-smiled at him.

"Grayson," Adrienne said. "Why don't you tell us about your tea plantation?"

"What would you like to know?"

"I've always wanted to go to India. It's so spiritual."

"Spiritual?" Grayson chuckled and, after an uncomfortable pause, continued. "People are people. No matter where they live. Sure, there are temples and mosques, and they bow and pray, dance and chant. That doesn't stop them from being human. Why, just this past year there was a sensational murder."

"Oh, tell us about it," Adrienne said. "I love true crime!"

"I'm not sure everyone shares your enthusiasm," Grayson said.

"Well, of course they do." Adrienne spoke so loudly I began to suspect she was more than a little drunk. "Keith's favorite book is *The Stranger Beside Me,* or at least it was, and Ro is a horrible writer. Oh my god, I mean horror writer. You know that's what I meant, right?"

I wasn't sure, but even I could see the humor in the moment.

"It isn't much of a story, really," Grayson said. "Just another man who murdered his wife and tried to make it look like an accident."

"He 'fell in love' with someone else, didn't he?" Adrienne made air quotes with her fingers, her nails painted a festive red.

"Technically, he'd been in love with her all along. The other woman, I mean. Yet for some reason, and this part is quite murky, he married someone else. They seemed happy. That's what people say."

"Then she showed up, right?"

"It seems it was chance. An accident. Almost impossible luck that they should have visited the Taj Mahal on the same day, the same hour, both bringing visitors from the west."

"Wasn't the Taj Mahal built as a testament to love?" I asked.

"Yes, it was," Keith said.

Grayson continued. "She had no idea of his true nature."

"Oh yeah, right." Adrienne had slipped out of her shoes and sat with her legs curled beneath her. The angrier she seemed, the more I liked her.

"By all accounts he was a very likable fellow."

"Until he murdered his wife."

"How did he do it?" I was always looking for new ways to kill someone, and felt quite excited when Grayson took a deep breath as if about to reveal something astounding. Instead, he relayed a rather prosaic account of a cut brake line, a trick I had already used, prompting a critic to note that my work had become "tired." Glancing at Keith, I saw fresh lines of stress etched on his face, his jaws clenched.

"This has been lovely," I said. "It must be the big meal, and the traveling. I feel so tired."

"I hope I didn't offend you," Grayson said, his tone flat.

"What? No. I usually go to bed early."

"Yes, well. Jovy will escort you to your rooms."

"Jovy?" Adrienne asked, and we exchanged a conspiratorial look, something between alarm, amusement, and conspiracy.

With a tilt of his head the old man leaned slightly forward, a bow of acquiescence.

"I hope you find your accommodations comfortable,"

Grayson said. "We can reconvene tomorrow. Christmas Eve. Such a magical time!"

Adrienne slipped on her shoes and Keith took a final sip of wine.

"Wasn't Jovy the name of the man in your story?" I asked. "Remember?"

"Well, of course I remember," Grayson said. "Jovy has been with my family since before I was born."

I nodded, somewhat cowed into silence by his incredulousness. The three of us filed out of the room past Grayson, who remained in his chair like a mafia don. We each paused before him to say good night. I heard him ask Adrienne if she had gotten enough to eat, and her expression, before she realized I was watching, was distressed. When I frowned in an exaggerated manner, my eyebrows raised, meaning to convey solidarity, she surprised me by hooking her arm in mine.

"So, now we just follow the crypt keeper into the dark, right," she whispered. "This is the part in the movie where I'd be shouting for the women to run."

"And Keith too," I said, eyeing his broad shoulders ahead of us.

Adrienne squeezed my arm. "Do you think he acted strange when Grayson told that story about the man murdering his wife?"

I don't know if Keith heard her, but he stopped right

then to wait for us.

The house was abundantly decorated with pine trees and boughs, the scent almost overwhelming. I had never believed that Grayson's father had allowed a fawn to roam free there, but as we began to ascend the wide, *Gone with the Wind* staircase, I realized anything was possible. The rich could afford eccentricities the rest of us saved for dreams and nightmares.

Jovy led us down the long hallway lit by the flickering candlelight of wall sconces, providing an effect that was either charming or menacing. I'd been distracted when I'd been upstairs earlier, wondering if I'd made a mistake by coming—there were so many closed doors and they were all the same, like a hotel without numbers—I was glad for the escort.

He stopped in front of a door and, with an elegant wave, invited Adrienne into her room. I glimpsed a purple suitcase with clothes tumbled out of it, and the dance of light that signified a fire in the hearth.

"If you please," he said, uttering the first words I'd heard from him in just the tone I would have written if he were a character, a slithering whisper of congeniality.

"Thank you, but I am going to accompany my friend to her room." Adrienne squeezed my arm again.

We continued to Keith's room where we all bade self-conscious good-nights. When I felt his gaze linger on me far longer than seemed necessary, Adrienne squeezed my arm again. I was not used to the secret language of friends and found it baffling, cloying, and slightly charming. When we arrived at my room I tried to discourage her, pleading exhaustion. "Thank you so much," she said to the old man, leaning into my shoulder to propel me forward, unlocking her arm to close the door behind us.

It was a perfect room right out of any horror story. There was a large, gothic window with diaphanous drapes drawn, and a massive bed covered with an ivory spread which had the texture of silk. A red velvet Christmas stocking hung from the mantel, dangling above the fire that shed mysterious shadows across Adrienne's face, causing her to look slightly Wyeth.

"Oh, my god. We need to talk about what we're going to do," she said, making herself comfortable in one of the two massive chairs positioned by the fire.

"Do?" I tried to remember what thread of conversation she was picking up.

"You see it too, right?"

"Adrienne, I'm sorry, I'm not—"

"I mean, when you think of it, we don't really know each other."

I nodded. It was true, and the fact that we had agreed to spend this holiday together struck me as extremely foolish. I shouldn't have been surprised. I had a talent for making bad choices, which often became fodder for my work. I asked my therapist once if I had been broken by what happened to me and she said everyone was broken, but some people were strong in the broken places. I told her I was not a fan of Hemingway. "I'm more a Stephen King kind of person," I said, and she looked at me as if I had suddenly turned into a zucchini.

"Ro? You okay?"

I shook my head to regain focus. "I think I might have had too much to drink. It's been a while."

"Oh? I thought you would enjoy drinking quite a bit. Don't get me wrong. You look good. I like the whole—you know—dark angel vibe. I could never pull it off, my-self. Too blonde, obviously. Here, sit." Adrienne pointed at the other chair as though she were the hostess, her shoes already on the floor, her feet tucked under her. I was not eager to engage in this slumber party behavior but quickly assessed that the easiest way to get through the inconvenience might be the worn path of least resis-tance. So I sat. Wind rattled the panes of glass and there was a faint sound beyond the drapes as though some-one were throwing sand at the windows. Hail, or a gritty snow at least. The storm comes in, raging like a beast, I thought, and immediately logged the phrase in a corner of my mind to write down later.

"Ro? Ro, are you listening?"

"Sorry. I sometimes space out."

Adrienne nodded solemnly. "Is it, you know, 'cause of what happened to your family?"

"What? No. I . . . Can you just repeat what you were saying?"

"I was saying how I had my suspicions. His behavior has always been off. Even when we were young."

"But I thought you two were a thing?"

"Me and Keith?"

"No not Keith. Grayson."

She shook her head. "Wow, Ro, you really didn't hear a thing I said, did you? Keith. I'm talking about Keith. There's something wrong with him."

"With Keith?"

"Yes."

"You don't . . . Grayson, sure. But Keith?"

"Oh, Grayson is harmless."

"Really? I mean I didn't know him like you did."

"Oh, believe me, Ro, Grayson has always been a freak." She smiled in a way that suggested pleasant memories before she waved her hand in front of her face. "Freaky for sure, but Keith—"

"He's in mourning, Adrienne."

"Well, that's what he wants you to think."

"What does that mean?"

"Didn't you see him? Didn't you see how he looked

when Grayson told that story about the man who killed his wife?"

"It was a pretty insensitive story to tell to a man whose wife just died in a car accident."

"Poor Lena."

"What are you implying?"

Adrienne's mascara-smudged eyes locked on mine. "Come on, Ro. You have to see it."

A log tumbled and threw off sparks. Happy to have something to do besides reason with a woman whose hold on reality seemed lax, I grabbed the poker, opened the grate, and set about invigorating the fire. It wasn't until I returned to my seat that I saw how Adrienne's expression was altered, her narrow eyebrows lowered, her red mouth a subtraction mark.

"You think I'm nuts, don't you?"

"What? No," I lied.

"She told me, though."

"What? Who?"

"Lena. Well, not told exactly. We wrote back and forth a bit once we found each other again. It took her awhile to admit it. Well, not admit it. She wasn't like that."

"Like what?"

"Direct. But I could tell. She was very unhappy. He didn't treat her right."

I wasn't sure how to respond. Though Lena certainly looked unhappy in every photograph I'd seen, that did not mean she was an abused wife as Adrienne seemed to be implying.

"Is this something you just started to suspect? I mean, you drove all the way here with him, didn't you?"

Adrienne eyed me as if I were a child she'd grown weary of sparring with. "I'm surprised at you, Ro. I expected better than this."

"Excuse me?"

"After what you've been through I thought you'd be more aware. I'll admit to being shocked when I first found out. Who would have guessed that the mousey girl I knew had been through something so intense? You changed quite a bit, you know, over the years. Now you wear it."

"Wear what?"

"You know." She waved her hand in my direction. "The horror."

I don't know why that made me feel embarrassed, seen in a way I hadn't been for a long time.

"P.I.," she said.

"What?"

She leaned forward. "Private investigator. That's what I do now."

"You're investigating me?"

She shook her head no, her lips pursed.

"Keith?"

She scanned the room. "Jesus, what I wouldn't give for a minibar. Oh, hey, you hung a stocking."

"No, it was here already. Listen, Adrienne. Maybe we both had too much to drink? Or we're tired. I know I am. Maybe this will look different in the morning."

"He has all your books. Lena told me. The short stories too, even the ones in weird little magazines no one can find. He found them. He has a special bookshelf dedicated just to you."

"Well." I had to turn my face away in order to hide my pleasure.

"He likes to quote passages of your work."

Horror writers run into this sort of shit all the time. People think any person who writes about monsters is one. Some believe that anyone who reads horror longs for bedlam. Apparently, Adrienne had concluded that dear, affable Keith had murdered his wife, based on the fact that he enjoyed my work.

What had I been thinking? How had I gotten myself into this ridiculous situation?

I knew it was only the play of shadows across her face, but too-blonde Adrienne, sitting there with her legs tucked beneath her, suddenly looked hideous. What was she capable of? I had no idea. I decided to proceed with caution.

"What should we do?" I asked, and her face immediately brightened.

"I was beginning to worry you didn't understand."

"Oh, I understand."

"Well, I thought you would. Considering what you write."

"So, what's the plan?"

"Just act normal."

I pretended to cough in order to cover the shock of a laugh trying to make its escape. That was her big plan? Act normal?

"Okay."

She nodded, eyeing me closely. "I'm not sure you are taking this seriously," she said, her blonde hair a sudden waterfall over her face as she leaned over to retrieve her shoes. "But I'm trying to help you." She straightened, tossed her hair back, and stood.

I pretended not to notice when she leaned toward me for a hug. "Be careful," she said, as I closed the door in her face, disappointed to discover it had no lock.

Just my luck, I thought. Finally a hero comes along, and it's Adrienne.

~

A particular challenge of being a horror writer is what we know. For instance, one out of every hundred people is a psychopath. The average person has run into quite a few, and sometimes they run into each other. People tend to confuse psychopaths with sociopaths but a sociopath, prone to rage and erratic behavior, has difficulty holding down a job or leading anything that resembles a normal existence, while the psychopath can go unrecognized for an entire lifetime. Not all psychopaths develop a murder practice. Contrary to common perception, some psychopaths are capable of loving in their own way and often suffer feelings of loneliness and despair that can lead to suicide. Others do quite well in politics and business where their ruthless tendencies are channeled into power and profits. Even those psychopaths who murder are capable of chilling self-control. The notorious Dennis Rader, otherwise known as the BTK killer (bind, torture, kill), terrorized Wichita, Kansas, for over three decades then took a ten-year hiatus. At the time there was speculation that BTK had died or was serving a prison sentence for some other crime while, in truth, he was always there, standing in line in the supermarket, washing his car in the driveway, greeting his neighbors at church.

It wasn't anything I liked to think about that night in the house I shared with virtual strangers (and a possible vampire), but I was almost positive Grayson was a psychopath, and beginning to think Adrienne might be as well. The question was what kind were they? Dangerous, or merely terrible?

I crawled under the covers, staring into the fire until my eyes burned, falling asleep like that, suddenly awoken by a figure standing near the hearth. The silhouette turned at my gasp.

"Keith?"

"Ro."

"What are you doing here?"

"I was trying to surprise you."

"Well, yeah, you surprised me. What the fuck?"

He stepped forward, and like a Victorian maiden, I pulled the comforter up under my chin.

"Oh, hey," he said. "I don't want . . . Oh, this was stupid. Don't be afraid. I was just putting something in your stocking. I'll go."

"What is it?"

"Excuse me?"

"What did you put in the stocking?"

"Do you want me to tell you?"

"Bring it," I said, noticing the thrilling convergence of anticipation and trepidation.

He extended the stocking to me with a straight arm.

"Oh, here." I scooted over and patted the mattress. He sat facing me, one leg dangling over the side as though we were a married couple in an old black-and-white movie.

"It's just a little thing," he said. "I wanted you to have it, but we agreed not to exchange gifts."

"This is really nice," I said, turning the stocking over. A candy cane, a chocolate Santa, an orange, and a small wrapped package fell into my lap.

"You don't have to open it now."

I unwrapped the box, opened it, and lifted out the ornament by its hook, a small carved deer to match the one he'd given me so long ago, though this one had an infinitesimal bell dangling from its antler, which I tapped with my finger, pleased when it jingled softly.

"I don't know if . . ."

"It's perfect," I said.

Keith leaned closer. Close as a kiss, I thought, my heart beating like a maniac.

"Do you want me to leave?"

Instead of speaking, I threw back the covers with a flourish.

"Like a bird," he mumbled.

"What?"

"Like a little bird just opened her wings."

"Get in here," I said, carefully placing the ornament on the bedside table.

The last timber of his chuckle was still in the air when his cold legs brushed mine, and his hot hand was on my breast, his lips against my neck breathing into me when I thought of Adrienne again. Would thrill and fear have merged when he grasped my wrists if not for her? He was a good man, I thought, as he snored softly against my throat. Closing my eyes I smelled the bright scent of the orange, which had landed beside my face. I was setting it on the table when Keith murmured.

"What?"

"Released of the body by the body," he said, pulling me closer to say it again. "Released of the body by the body."

Just like she said. Like it was a bad thing that he loved my work enough to memorize the lines I had written. I closed my eyes to hold on to that feeling, and the next thing I knew I was awoken by an icy light, squinting at Keith, who was dressed and standing by the door.

"Are you sneaking out?"

He shook his head no as he walked back to me.

"Merry Christmas Eve," he said.

I nodded. Sleepy. Happy. Confused. "Is it my breath?"

"What? No," he laughed.

"Come on, Keith; don't make me drag it out of you."

"Right." He sat on the edge of the bed, hitched himself closer. "It's Adrienne."

"Yeah?"

"She . . . I think she . . . Oh, god this sounds so seventh grade, but I think she likes me."

"Really?"

"Some of the things she said on the way here. I didn't know. Believe me. I wouldn't have agreed to carpool with her if I thought . . . Anyway, I am not sure she's all there, if you know what I mean. I find her a little frightening, to be honest. I don't want to upset her."

"No. I don't think we want to upset Adrienne."

His face was so close I might have counted freckles, instead I studied his eyes, which were pale spokes of green, blue, and brown.

"She sleeps in her bed, dreaming of gingerbread, never guessing who watches in the dark," he said.

I couldn't stop grinning. Not while I showered, and not as I dressed. Not when I sat at the table laden with an enormous spread of pastries, bread, assorted cheese, iridescent jellies in crystal bowls, whipped butter, glass pitchers of various juices, and a platter of chocolate-covered strawberries.

I didn't even stop smiling when Keith greeted me with a polite, "Good morning," giving no indication there was anything between us other than two decades and a long table. In fact, it only made me want to smile more. How delicious, the taste of secrets.

"Good morning, Ro." Grayson greeted me from his end of the table, his lips unusually pink in the bright light that streamed through the grand windows behind him framing the vast property smothered in white. "I trust you slept well? You certainly look rested."

"Oh, I tossed around a bit," I said, maintaining my composure as Keith fumbled with his butter knife. "But once I settled down, slept better than I have in a long while. Where's Adrienne?"

"She appears to be a late sleeper. As I told Keith, you should go ahead and eat. We don't have to be formal."

I scanned the room for signs of anything suggesting informal, besides my attire. A fire blazed, the chandelier was lit, and Grayson sat in a chair so elaborate it looked like a throne.

"Jovy would be happy to prepare eggs to your specification," Grayson said, beckoning in the direction of a dark corner, and the old man stepped out, startling me. Perhaps because my mood was already inclined toward mirth, I laughed and waved him away. Without a change of expression, he took tiny backward steps.

"Someone seems particularly cheerful this morning," Grayson said.

I glanced at Keith just long enough to catch him eyeing me with one brow raised. "Looks like the weather is clearing up," he said.

"Only a temporary lull," Grayson said, quite focused on pulling apart a croissant with his long fingers.

"Really?" I was skeptical, but even as I spoke, flakes

began to tumble down from the gray sky, and that, for some reason, did the trick. I was no longer smiling. I didn't understand it, myself. After all, I had abandoned my plan for an early departure. Yet as the flurry quickened to a fall, it was almost as though I could hear each one land, a cacophony of dread.

"Maybe I should check on Adrienne."

"Don't," Keith said. "I mean, if she needs her sleep, I think we shouldn't disturb her."

"I'm afraid I have a little unexpected business I must attend to this morning," Grayson said. "Would you like tea?"

Jovy had returned, pushing an old-fashioned tea cart before him.

"But it's Christmas Eve," I said.

"Can't be helped. It isn't a holiday for everyone, you know."

Jovy approached Keith, but he waved him away.

Not, generally, a tea drinker myself, I pretended enthusiasm for the brew Jovy poured for me, surprised by a Mona Lisa smile that broke through his stony countenance.

"It smells like woodsmoke," I said, charmed by the tiny, dollhouse-sized pitcher of cream, the miniature tongs, and small silver bowl filled with brown and white sugar cubes.

"So, as I was saying, I hope you accept my apologies. Jovy"—Grayson paused to watch his cup of tea make its trembling arrival—"will be available to see to your comfort. Please make yourself at home." He poured cream into his tea, dropped three sugar cubes in it, and stirred. "The library is quite cozy on a winter's day."

"I was thinking of taking a walk," Keith said. "Doing a little exploring."

"Jovy can outfit you with snowshoes, if you like."

"Yeah, sure, that would be great. Maybe you'd like to join me?" he asked, continuing at my nod. "I'm going to change into warmer clothes. Grayson, this has been a spectacular breakfast. Thank you."

"Of course. I am happy to provide you with some solace during this first challenging holiday without your beloved."

Keith pushed away from the table and trudged out of the room in a display of emotion I thought bordered on overacting. For a few moments the room was still but for the crackling fire.

"Well, this is fortunate. I'm pleased to have some time alone with you," Grayson said.

"I thought you had a meeting."

"Yes, a call. I have a few minutes."

"Good," I said, which was a lie. As bountiful as the table was, as festive as the decorations, an uncomfortable atmosphere emanated from Grayson. "This tea is lovely."

"I'm so glad you're enjoying it. We save it for rainy days and winter storms."

Desperate for something to say, I found myself sharing how the smoky aroma reminded me of camping.

"Is that something you did with your family?"

"Yes." While it is true that I had shared the tragedy in interviews for years, I did so in generalized terms after the time I had relayed private details with a reporter because I'd mistaken his interest as personal. I told him about the Christmas poems my mother recited, my father's penchant for the obscure genre of historical humor, my brother's fascination with insects. The reporter wrote all about it, neglecting to understand that those details had not been meant for general consumption. After that, others only wanted more. ("Did your mother memorize poems for other seasons?" "So, your father had a quirky sense of humor, I suppose that explains your name?" "Do you wonder if your brother would have become an entomologist?") Until my memories were so depleted of any life force they could have belonged to anyone.

"I want you to know I forgave you long ago."

"Excuse me?"

"I will admit I was disappointed for quite a while. I kept checking the mail, wondering if it had been lost."

"Grayson, what are you—"

"But Christmas came and went, New Year's too. I finally accepted that you never sent my gift."

"Oh, I—"

"It was disappointing, of course. It was an exchange, wasn't it? I had your name and sent you—"

"The bell."

"Yes. The bell."

"It was a terrific gift, Grayson."

"I'm glad to hear you appreciated it."

"I didn't mean to . . . I am really bad about shit like this."

"So what was it? My present, I mean?"

"Five dollars. I stole it from Keith's coat pocket. That was the point. Remember? We were supposed to steal something? I thought I was so clever. I wanted everyone to see how funny it was. I meant it as a good laugh."

"But you kept it."

"I didn't think it would matter. I mean, I assumed you had enough."

"That was the Christmas my father was dying. I might have enjoyed a laugh."

"I'm sorry, Grayson. You're right. Of course. I didn't mean anything by it."

He waved his hand, flicking away my words as though they were flies. "As I said. I forgave you long ago."

Though clearly he hadn't. I looked out the window at the falling snow.

"So what became of my bell? Do you ring it often?"

I shook my head. "It's silly, I suppose, but I wrapped it up in the glove, and put it back in the box."

"You still have it, though?"

"Yes," I said.

"Why?"

I shrugged.

"Why would you keep a bell you never ring?"

"I know it probably sounds silly. But I thought I might need it. You know, to call a Krampus. Like the one in your story." I thought this might brighten the mood, instigate a chuckle. Instead, Grayson nodded solemnly.

"Be careful," he said. "You can't control them when they come."

Well, what had I been thinking? Even all those years ago, Grayson had been a strong storyteller. I decided to play along.

"So, what happens when the Krampus come?"

"Mayhem. Chaos. You know."

"Is there any way to stop them?"

"Some people believe feeding them helps. It causes a distraction, at least. But you can't stop them from their nature. It would be like trying to stop the snow from falling by leaving bread out on the porch."

Jesus, Grayson might have had a life in fiction, if he'd wanted it. Still, I saw a flaw in his account. "What about all the bells? The church bells, the ones in Christmas songs? Wedding bells? The little bell some child rings?"

"What about them?"

"Well, obviously ..." And here we were interrupted by Keith's return, bounding into the room like a golden retriever.

"I'm afraid I let the time get away from me," Grayson said, pushing his chair back to stand.

"But, wait."

"Yes?"

"I just ..." What did it matter? Yet I had to know. "What about all those bells ringing and no monster comes?"

"My dear," Grayson said, standing with one hand on his chair. "You, of all people, know."

"What?"

"They come."

~

Jovy outfitted us with snowshoes and a small backpack in which he placed a thermos of hot cocoa, two breakdown plastic cups, and sandwiches. He did all this wordlessly, his movements unhurried.

The last thing he did was produce our phones, removing them from his pocket as we stood in the front yard. We were dressed for the snow, but he only wore his usual outfit of white shirt beneath black jacket, cotton trousers, and dress shoes. His shoulders already sported a snowy landscape, his tremor so pronounced I had to concentrate to fix my hand on the phone.

You may recall my novel *Have You Seen Marla?*, set in the stunning wilderness of Sequoia National Park where, every year or so, a visitor goes missing. There are rumors of Sasquatch, aliens, and persistent speculation about a serial killer, which I used as inspiration, but the fact is, people don't realize how easy it is to become lost. I was very grateful to Jovy for understanding that we might need such assistance.

Keith, who had begun immediately jabbing his finger at his phone, pronounced with great excitement that it worked, and Jovy abruptly turned to look over his shoulder. I told Keith to put the phone away. "I don't think Grayson knows we have them."

Jovy turned back to meet my gaze. He was, without exaggeration, the whitest man I'd ever seen, the snow that landed on his face almost indistinguishable from his complexion.

"You're shivering," I said. "You should go inside."

He did the strangest thing. He lifted his icy hand and pointed toward the road. Before I could ask for clarification, he pivoted back toward the house, forging an effortless trail through the heavy snow, which seemed to melt beneath his feet as if he burned like a devil or a saint.

A flicker of light in an upstairs window caught my attention. Grayson, watching. I pretended good cheer and waved; he raised his hand in response, then stepped back into the shadows.

"I didn't think we'd be able to get a signal out here," Keith said. "I can't believe our luck."

It was the first time I really doubted him. Could anyone be more naïve? Then, of course, I doubted myself. Could anyone be more cynical?

Snowflakes stuck to Keith's pale eyelashes and eyebrows. He smiled and reached for my mittened hand. We tried to walk like that, but the snowshoes made it impossible. I led us down the drive toward the road.

"I think Jovy wants us to leave," I said.

"What?" Keith chuckled. "Yeah, he probably does."

"No. I mean, really. I think we are in trouble."

Keith stopped, looking at me with his head cocked as if I had suddenly become misshapen.

"I think Grayson might have done something to Adrienne."

"Done something?"

"Don't look at me like that. I'm serious, Keith."

"I'm sorry."

"What are you sorry about?"

"I know what happened when you were young made you like this. Hey, hey, Ro. Stop."

It is very difficult to walk quickly in snowshoes, though I tried. Plopping over the snow like some maladjusted jackrabbit. I might have kept on had Keith not fallen, and the sight of him, waving his arms and legs like a beetle on its back, stifled my rage.

"I am not," I said as I stomped over to him, "broken."

"All right, all right, can you—"

"I am not."

"Ro, I am sorry. Of course you aren't. It's me," he said, pointing to his heart. "I'm the broken one."

I reached out to pull him up, but when that didn't work, extended the other hand and thought, for a moment, that I was going to fall on top of him and we would turn into a Hallmark movie, but he finally managed to rise to a stand.

"Do you want to call the police?"

"Yes," I said, and then, "wait."

"What, Ro?"

"Maybe we should look around a little first. I don't want to make the mistake of ignoring this, but I also don't want to make a big deal if it is nothing."

Keith had taken out his phone and was squinting at it. "Well, that's good, 'cause I lost the signal," he said, following me as if I was not doing the stupid thing people do in bad movies. I took a hard left off the snow-covered road, through the bank of pines, back onto the property, so far from the house all that could be seen of it was chimney smoke.

I admit I had no real plan. Later, when this story was told, it seemed I knew what I was looking for, that everything happened by intention when, in reality, it was just luck. Stomping around on the snow, which continued to fall in salty flakes, flailing, really, with no direction in mind, not sure how to proceed or even what I was looking for while Keith kept checking his phone, it occurred to me, in my vague unfocused state, that he might be frightened of this person I'd become, this irrational creature, but then I saw the snow-covered steeple from which rose a tarnished cross, and I knew everything Grayson had told us all those years ago was not fantasy, but confession. Keith cursed softly and said, "You don't think . . . ?" But I didn't wait for him to finish. I made my way to the small church boarded up like a haunted house, or a prison of some kind, a padlocked chain drawn through the handles of the large double gothic door.

"We can pick the lock," Keith said. "Do you have, you

know, one of those things in your hair?"

"Like a bobby pin?" I asked. "No, I don't have a bobby pin."

But I have written enough stories to know there is always a way out or in and, as I looked for a solution, discovered the old church was shedding stone like a creature's skin.

I tried not to be bothered by how Keith cowered when I returned to the door and raised that rock overhead as if he was afraid I would kill him. I drove it down on the lock and when my arms grew tired he took over, and I thought I could hear muffled screams, which caused me to wonder if I had fallen out of my love story back into a horror of my own mind, but Keith said, "Do you hear that?" and I knew then that if I was lost, so were we both, and if I had fallen, we had fallen together, and the lock broke open and we drew out the chain, and opened the door, revealing a sanctuary in shadows, immediately hushed by the dark, and, in spite of the boarded stained glass and dusty pews and altar askew beneath a giant cross, I felt—temporarily—assured, as if something good resided there that would protect me, until the feeling was shattered by a scream.

"I'm going to call the cops," Keith said. "Ro, wait."

But I could not. I was drawn to it, summoned, you might say, though I cannot tell you if it was the beckoning of evil or good. Whatever it was, I could not resist it. I walked up the nave while Keith continued tapping on his phone. "Ro, wait."

I crossed in front of the altar to enter a narrow hallway, so dark I needed my phone as a lantern to guide me down, just as Grayson had gone as a boy. The walls were filled with Krampus, standing on two legs like men, obscene tongues, dragging chains, hooves, horns and claws, eyes widened with rage.

The path narrowed, the ceiling so low I had to bow, imagining myself a girl of sixteen, returned home early to rescue her family. I heard a sound, like the rattling of chains, and that scream again, and I was drawn to the light, not a blaze, but a gray light within the widening passage, frightened when I heard footsteps behind me, reassured when he said, "It's just me, Ro. The police are coming," and I stepped from the narrow dark into a room lined with monsters, drawn and painted. And bones. So many bones. And, in the corner, locked in a cage, Adrienne.

Her nails were broken, her eyes wild, her hair all tangles as though she was becoming one of them. She wept and pleaded and babbled. You cannot imagine how much can be taken from a person. Keith left to ring the church bell to guide the police, the sound so loud I felt it inside me, as if I'd swallowed the reverberation. What I could not undo for my family, I undid for Adrienne. I stayed with her until the police came, and I held her hand through the bars as they sawed them, and when she was released she sprang into my arms as if we were best friends, sisters, or lovers, and I held her like that all the way out.

The snow had stopped falling, and everywhere I looked was a winter wonderland; the kind of world children dream of on Christmas Eve. They wrapped us in silver blankets, and when the sun broke, it lit us like angels with folded wings.

~

A year later, we had a Christmas wedding. When well-meaning people suggested it seemed rushed, I explained that we'd known each other for two decades. Others said, "He's your prince, isn't he? He rescued you." But he didn't. I rescued myself, and we rescued Adrienne. Still, I was pleased to inspire a love story, for once.

I was completely surprised when I discovered I was pregnant. Peering at the menopause horizon, I couldn't have been more shocked to find my womb occupied by fairies, stunned by tears of joy when the ultrasound revealed a shadowy shape of the fetus. It was early enough that I barely showed, not that it would have mattered, except I had found my lace wedding dress in a resale shop which, a month later, would not have fit.

We chose a small, nondenominational chapel used mostly by pagans and Unitarians, saving a bundle on flowers because the space was already decorated for the season. We kept the guest list small. I had no family, and Keith's parents had died years before. He said he was not close to his other relatives. That's what he said. He never told me they disapproved, but I had my suspicions. After all, I am no Lena.

Even though Adrienne had accepted our invitation, I didn't think she would come, but she pushed her way into the dressing room where I waited with Mags, my maid of honor/publicist, breaking my bliss as easily as if it were a spider's web.

She looked lovely, but something wasn't right. It exuded from her like a bad perfume.

"You can't do this, Ro," she said. "It's a mistake."

I asked Mags to leave and, when she looked uncertain, assured her I would be fine.

"Well, okay, but I'm standing right outside the door. You shout if you need anything. Don't fuck up this day for her," she said as she passed Adrienne.

"How are you?" I asked. "I'm so glad you could come."

"Stop. Don't talk to me like this."

"Like what?"

"You know. Like I'm crazy. I'm not."

"I'm sorry," I said, and meant it. "Believe me, I understand. It's just . . . it's only been a year. There hasn't even been a trial yet. I think you've been affected by this more than you realize."

"He's evil, Ro. I don't know why you can't see it."

"Who? Who are we talking about?"

"Keith."

"He saved your life, Adrienne."

"What does that have to do with anything? God, Ro, how can you be so naïve? Don't you realize that evil people are fully capable of doing good things? I mean, how do you think they hide in plain sight? They wear a mask of normal. I thought you understood this. I'm so disappointed in you. You're as bad as that old man. That Jovy."

"What are you talking about? Did they find him?"

She shook her head no, her blonde hair catching the light.

"What do you . . . ? Adrienne, this is my wedding. I don't want to do this right now."

"You're like him, because he stayed there all those years, knowing what that family was up to."

"But I thought you told the police it was only Grayson? Adrienne, Jovy helped save your life. You know that, right? He gave us our phones."

"Why can't you see what is happening right in front of your face, Ro? I'm telling you that you are in danger.

I'm warning you."

"I think it's time for you to leave."

"I won't. I will stand up and object."

I believed her too. Will you believe me when I say I wasn't angry? I really did understand. Once a person goes through something so terrible, perceptions are changed; even love is altered.

"Mags," I called. I didn't have to say it again. She came into the room with her brother, who covered Adrienne's mouth as he dragged her out the side door, then waited to watch her drive away. He remained at the back of the church for the ceremony, but she didn't return. It was only later that I realized how much our little chapel was like the one she had been held captive in and wondered if that might have triggered her.

Still, we decided not to send her a birth announcement, or a change of address when we moved out of the place I'd bought as a single woman (too full of sharp edges, a balcony but no yard) into our new home where we spent our first Thanksgiving eating Chinese take-out surrounded by unpacked boxes even as I secretly wondered if there was something wrong with me that nothing could fix. Did I want too much? Was I setting impossible standards by feeling that Keith was both cloyingly attentive and disappointingly distant? Why had I been in such a hurry to get married, anyway? It was like

I'd been put under a spell. I confided in Mags and she said, "You were. It's called love. Don't worry; lots of people go through this after the honeymoon is over." I tried to convince myself that all we needed was time, but there were moments when I wondered if Adrienne had been right. Fucking Adrienne; even from afar she kept getting in my head, making me doubt my own happiness.

He made perfect blueberry pancakes, knew how to set up all our electronics, bought excellent wine and good cheese. He painted the baby's room and, when I said the green was too dark, painted it again and got it right. He was an excellent birthing coach, completely nonplussed by the drama, though once we were all home together, I wished he was more proactive as a father. He did everything I asked, but I began to resent his inability to see for himself what needed to be done. When I complained, he told me he was unhappy with his work. He wanted to make a career change, get out of sales. He left the house regularly to meet with investors, or advisers. I was never sure, exactly, but couldn't imagine anything duller than selling insurance, so I supported him even as I resented it. After all, when was I supposed to get my writing done? I briefly considered hiring a nanny but, probably because of all the diabolical nanny movies I had watched over the years, dismissed the idea as too frightening.

He was gone that afternoon, the baby asleep, when

I decided to pull out the Christmas decorations, my meager assortment and several large boxes filled with a distressing amount of Lena's things. I started a trash bag for most of it, not to be mean, but I had married her husband not her.

I was feeling cranky, annoyed that Keith had not taken care of this task, near the bottom of another stash of creepy snowmen and leering penguins when my hand brushed what I recognized as a card box. I could hear the baby's wake-up noises through the monitor, and I thought, *You don't have to look.*

This doesn't mean anything, I told myself, staring at the picture on the lid of a little bear holding a red flower. It was just the sort of thing Lena would have liked. Many such boxes of cards must have been sold. Adrienne had gotten into my head. I opened the box filled with that stupid bear with its stupid flower. I told myself not to open the card, but I did open the card, and inside was blank. I opened the next one too, and the next. The baby was crying but I wanted an answer, something definitive, that's what I told myself. Then, just as I heard the door open, and him calling my name, I came to the last card. Different than all the rest, a picture of an idyllic winter scene, a little house in the snow, all the windows lit, and the drawing of a face, a frightened girl looking at me from my own past; inside, beneath the printed "Merry Christmas," my signature.

"Ro, Ro? Are you all right?" He stepped into the room, the baby in his arms. "Jesus, Ro, I thought. Oh."

"Give him to me."

"You have to let me explain."

"Give me my baby."

For a terrifying moment I thought I was going to watch my husband smother our child but, instead, he kissed the little forehead and then, like a decent man, handed him over.

"Ro."

"Get out."

"Right," he said, backing up to sit in the chair, as if we were about to have a pleasant end-of-the-day conversation. "Actually, this is a good thing."

"A good thing?" I asked, and realized I felt stuck. I tried to make sense of what was happening, but the pieces would not connect.

"I've wanted to talk about this for a while."

The baby began to whimper again, and I realized I was holding him too tight, pressed hard against my crazy heart.

"Ro, listen to me. It was a mistake."

"A mistake?"

Keith leaned back, staring past me with a contemplative gaze. "You know how teenagers are. I thought I had it all figured out. I saw how they treated you that day in the mall. I couldn't believe Mr. Syger would treat one of his own children like that."

"Wait. You knew my father?"

"I mean, all you wanted to do was go to a movie."

"Were you one of my father's students?"

He smiled. Proud of me. "Well, I was never in his class. We moved out of the district after one semester, and what happened at your house was a couple years later. I didn't expect him to recognize me. I only wanted to scare them."

What to do, what to do, what to do? I couldn't figure it out. "Why?"

"You were supposed to come home and rescue them, Ro! Who stands in the freezing snow that long, waiting for a stranger?"

"I don't understand."

"I just wanted to scare them. Tie them up. Just for show, you know?"

"This is—" I caught myself. Nuts, I thought, but didn't say.

"Everything was going great once I got that dog taken care of."

"Sampson?"

"I had your brother put him in the bathroom. He actually tried to escape. Your brother that is, but of course

I stopped him. After that, everyone behaved quite well. I was just about to leave when your father said my name."

I closed my eyes, as if that could prevent my hearing.

"You understand, don't you, Ro? I had to change the plan once he recognized me. It was all so innocent, but I knew no one would see it that way."

"Innocent?"

"I told him I was sorry when I lit the match."

"And then you left?"

"I had to. I couldn't exactly wait around, could I? I went out the back door, cut through your neighbor's yard to get my car which I had parked one street over. I guess I got lucky 'cause no one saw me. But I saw you."

"What?"

"Yep. At first I thought you were already gone, 'cause you weren't anywhere by the gazebo, but then I saw you, Ro, my beautiful girl, waiting in the snow. I couldn't stop, of course. I'd ruined everything before it even started."

"So you stalked me?" I realized I was rocking, gently, side to side, soothing my baby and myself.

He slumped a little, disappointed. "Ro, honey, you have a way of making yourself the center of every story. It's something you might want to work on. I felt bad about how things went. I moved on. I mean I didn't even know you were a student at UW."

"And Dell's? Meeting in Dell's?"

"It was just luck."

"I don't believe you."

He shrugged. "Once we finally talked, I realized you were kind of depressing . . . and, you know, dark. Oh, hey, don't look so upset. We were young. I didn't know myself very well. I didn't know what I wanted. Back then, I thought I needed someone like Lena. Someone, you know, good. Not like us."

"Like us?"

"But over the years, I came to understand I had been wrong about everything. Lena could never really know me, while you—"

"What?"

"You wrote about me all the time."

"I didn't."

"Ro, it's all right. Don't you see? You can be yourself with me."

"But you're a monster," I said.

He closed his eyes as if I had become unbearable. "All I ever tried to do was give you what you wanted."

"I want you to get out."

He stood and came toward me. I told myself to remain calm but when he reached as if to touch my shoulder, I screamed as though his hand was made of fire. The baby started crying again and my own tears blinded my vision but, even all this time later, I still see that look of pained astonishment on his face and, fucked up as it is, every time I remember—in the midst of my rage—I feel a stab of sorrow.

He left, not slamming the door, but softly closing it. I locked all the locks as if he didn't have keys of his own and called the police. They came to take my report then came back the next morning to tell me they had found his car by the bridge and, later, his corpse in the icy water.

Everyone says how lucky I am—the luckiest person who ever lived—to have survived a home invasion, a serial killer, and a psychopath husband. Who has luck like that? I do.

Lucky to watch my beautiful baby boy grow into the sort of toddler strangers comment on at the supermarket, calling him a little angel. Lucky to finally sell the house I'd bought when I still believed in the fantasy of us, and very lucky that after sitting for so long without a buyer, the low offer I made on Grayson's estate was accepted. Many people are superstitious about living in a place with such horrific history, but horror feels like home to me, this once lucky girl grown into a very lucky woman.

So lucky that when Jovy appeared at the front door one evening to offer his services, I didn't even think twice. It's an enormous place and I was happy to accept his help. He keeps the fires going, and the pantry stocked. He tends to the massive property, including the garden planted where the church once stood. All that, and he is a wonderful babysitter too. My son adores him. I am finally able to write again.

Every so often I am visited by a detective. They come from all over the country with their pictures of missing girls and dead women, looking for answers I don't have. All of them believe Keith must have killed more than we know. The mind reels to think of it, but after they leave, I write notes about our conversation, material for my new novel, filled with jagged wounds and blood. Humming carols as I work.

This, our first Christmas here, I try to give my son a holiday full of traditions like the kind normal families have. Like a character in a fairy tale, I banish all the bells, instructing Jovy not to allow any into the house, entrusting him with the old pencil box and its foul instrument, asking him to destroy it. My son is four years old now. The time for enchantment already grows narrow. I want him to have the experience of wonder before his capacity for it is ruined by life's dark truths.

We make sugar cookies, and decorate gingerbread, find a beautiful tree in the forest which we decorate with the ornaments I've had since I was young, the salt dough "Baby's first Christmas" and the rest, so long in my possession I can almost believe they have always been mine, tokens of an ordinary life.

We save the wooden deer to hang last. "Daddy?" our child asks, and I nod my head, yes.

"Your father was a monster," I say. My son raises his hands beside his head, fingers curled like claws, makes a frightening face, and we laugh.

On Christmas Eve, with reports of an approaching storm, the old house grows shadows I drive away with candlelight. We drink hot cocoa by the fire and I tell ghost stories, some of which are true. Before bed, we set out the cookie plate for Santa Claus, waking up on Christmas morning to the crumbs and a dark stench in the air that dissipates with the aroma of fresh pastries, coffee, and bread. Jovy has prepared a feast he sets out upon the table, platters of fruit and meat, towers of nuts and candy.

"But who will eat all this?" I ask, just as my boy comes running into the room, pencil box in one hand, bell in the other. I lurch toward him, and he mistakes it for a game, running away from me, ringing the old bell that grows louder and louder, echoing against the walls. "Jovy, what have you done?" I shout and his lips part with his piercing grin as the whole house shakes with the crashing of thunder, the clang and jangle of Christmas morning, the riotous noise of the storm that comes in, raging like a beast.

Acknowledgments

Sometimes our inner light goes out, but it is blown again into flame by an encounter with another human being. Each of us owes the deepest thanks to those who have rekindled this inner light.

Albert Schweitzer

Ellen also reached out to many authors, most of whom I have never met, to ask them to read this novella and, if so inclined, write some kind words about it. So many did, and I am forever grateful to all of them. Thank you Nathan Ballingrud, Laird Barron, Christopher Golden, Daryl Gregory, Joshilyn Jackson (my wonderful teacher), Alma Katsu, Sarah Langan, Benjamin Percy, Steve Rasnic Tem, A. C. Wise. Anyone looking for what to read next is guaranteed to find something great by seeking out the work of these writers.

I am fortunate to have had so many people in my life who have been so generous with their support of my odd hours, strange days, and love of the imaginary world. Thank you.

Rietje Marie Angkuw

Cathy Barber

Christopher Barzak

Bill Bauerband (my amazing husband)

Mary and Matt Bauerband

Jeremy Brett

Thomas Canty

Libby Collins

C. S. E. Cooney

Haddayr Copley-Woods

Terry Curtis

Joe, Peggy and Scott Deheck

Jean Beth Dole

Kathy and Jon Dopkeen

Faceout Studio

Meg Galarza

Emily Goldman

Marcia Gorra-Patek

Gavin Grant

Vince Haig

Marty Halpern

Michael Kelly

Mary Anne Kenney

Andrew King

Mary Leanord

Tithi Luathong

Brandon and Monica Luedtke

Lyons Family

Andrew Marshall

Anya Martin

Craig and Susan McCann

Liz Musser

Eileen Rickert

Jeanne Rickert

Katie Rickert

Michael Rickert

Sofia Samatar

Dax Schwartz

Greg and Michelle Spehr

David Surface

Gordon Van Gelder

Andrew Young

About the Author

Before earning her MFA from Vermont College of Fine Arts, **M. RICKERT** worked as kindergarten teacher, coffee shop barista, Disneyland balloon vendor, and personnel assistant in Sequoia National Park. She has published three short story collections, *Map of Dreams, Holiday,* and *You Have Never Been Here.* Her first novel, *The Memory Garden,* was published in 2014, and won the Locus Award. Her second novel, *The Shipbuilder of Bellfairie,* was published in 2021. She is the winner of the Crawford Award, World Fantasy Award, and Shirley Jackson Award. She currently lives in Cedarburg, Wisconsin.

TOR·COM

**Science fiction. Fantasy. The universe.
And related subjects.**

*

More than just a publisher's website, *Tor.com* is a venue for **original fiction, comics,** and **discussion** of the entire field of SF and fantasy, in all media and from all sources. Visit our site today—and join the conversation yourself.